I0624439

New Roots Farm Books – Book 2

BEE A GOOD STEWARD

Rubee's Happy Hive Series

Written by

Heidi Fowler

Illustrated by

A.C. DeMuth

To my father, Anthony DeMuth, who spends so much of his time creating the perfect illustrations for my books. I'm extremely thankful for the hard work he puts in and the dedication he has for supporting my stories with his wonderful gift.

ISBN: 978-1-960858-70-2

Published in the United States of America by:
Cobb Publishing
704 E. Main St.
Charleston, AR 72933
CobbPublishing.com
Editor@CobbPublishing.com

BEE
A GOOD
STEWARD

Rubee saw the sunlight fill the cracks of her hive. The new day was here! She was now three days old and, though that might not seem like much to you, for a bee it means a lot! Rubee stretched all of her legs and began looking for Beeatrice. Today she would start her new job! She was done with housekeeping and couldn't wait to find out what her next task would be.

After searching for a few minutes, she found Beeatrice talking with an older bee that Rubee had never met. "Yes ma'am, I'll be ready to leave as soon as I get Rubee started on her new job."

"Good morning, Beeatrice!" sang Rubee. "I'm so excited to do something new! I'm tired of cleaning all of these cells!" Rubee made a face as she looked around at the many cells on the frame on which she stood.

Beeatrice smiled at the young bee. "Remember Rubee, all of the work that we do is important. Not all jobs are pleasant, but we have to keep in mind that they are all necessary to keep the hive running properly." Beeatrice was rubbing her forelegs together nervously.

Rubee closed all of her eyes and listened to the hum of her many sisters working busily in the hive. The queen had been working long hours laying so many eggs that the population in her colony had exploded. Rubee's thoughts were interrupted when someone bumped into her, almost knocking her over. Her eyes flew open as one of her sisters yelled over her shoulder, "Please excuse me! I'm late to work!"

Rubee frowned. "It's getting crowded in here," she mumbled as she followed Beeatrice past the cells of brood.

"Yes. It is. In fact, I've heard talk of a possible swarm." Beeatrice was talking so low that Rubee could barely hear her, and she looked so worried.

Brood—Young bees that have not come out of their cells yet.

Rubee was quiet. She watched Beeatrice as the two squeezed through sisters and the occasional brother. She wondered why Beatrice was acting so strangely. She wanted to question her sister further, but couldn't work up the courage. They were walking through a part of the hive that she had never been to before and soon Rubee became occupied with all of the new things she was seeing. The cells around her did not hold baby bees. Instead, each cell held pollen, all different colors! Some displayed yellow, some had orange, and some were packed full of beautiful blue and purple.

"Look at all of the colors!" Rubee was amazed.

Pollen—Colored powder made by some types of plants.

Beeatrice stopped to look around. She had grown used to seeing the rainbow of pollen in these cells. She smiled. "It is beautiful, isn't it?" She looked down sadly.

Rubee couldn't stand it any longer. "Beeatrice, what is the matter?"

Beeatrice sniffed, "I'm just a little nervous Rubee. I start my new job today as well. Today I will leave the hive and begin foraging."

Rubee's big eyes grew even bigger. "You'll be leaving? You won't be here with me during the day anymore?"

"No, Rubee. Time goes quickly and we must make the most of it. It is important that we be good stewards of our time."

"Stewards? What is a steward?" Rubee scratched her head with her foreleg.

"A steward is someone who manages or looks after something that belongs to someone else," Beeatrice explaned.

"But, if a steward looks after something that belongs to someone else, why are we stewards of our own time?" Rubee was confused.

Beeatrice smiled. "Rubee, our time doesn't belong to us alone." She spread her forelegs outward toward the colony. "Our time belongs to our whole family because we have a job to do together. If even one of us misuses our time, the effects are felt by everyone here."

Rubee looked about. She looked at the cells filled with a rainbow of colors. She took in the multitude of bees working in every space around her. Everyone was busy doing something. Everyone had a purpose. She nodded, "I understand, Beeatrice. If I didn't clean the cells, the queen couldn't lay eggs, and there would be nowhere for baby bees to be born."

"Yes! Our time does belong to us, but it also belongs to each other and, above all, to God." Beeatrice looked down at Rubee who again looked confused. "God blessed us with life, little sister. He gave each of us a certain time here on earth to complete our tasks. We are to use that time to honor Him and do His will."

As this sunk in Rubee nodded. "Yes, our time is very important. Now I see how important it is."

Colony—a family of bees living in the same hive.

Will of God—God's plan for how we should live our lives.

The two had made it to the end of the frame they were on. Beeatrice turned to face Rubee. "Are you ready to start your new job?"

"Yes!" Rubee was excited to be doing something new. Even though she understood how important her first job had been, she was ready to move on.

Beeatrice took in a breath and led Rubee around the edge to the back side of the frame. Rubee looked around. She saw a few other young bees hauling something across the hexagon-patterned wall before her. "What is that?" she exclaimed.

Hexagon—A shape made up of six sides and six angles.

"Those are bees that have passed away, Rubee. All of our lives here on earth will end one day. This is one reason it is so important to be good stewards of our time. We could leave this life at any time. We never know when it is time for us to go."

Rubee was saddened by this. She had not thought before about any of the sisters and brothers around her leaving for good. "Beeatrice, I don't want you to become a forager. Please stay here with me! What if something happens to you out there?" She couldn't bear the thought of losing her older sister even for part of a day, let alone forever.

Beeatrice smiled and hugged the small bee. "Everything will be fine, Rubee. Don't be afraid! God takes care of us all. When it is time for us to go, we won't be alone; He will be with us. This life is only temporary. We are here only for a little while. But while we are here, we must work hard at our jobs while being the best we can be. We must serve God and each other. And that is why we are here on this frame. Your new job is undertaking."

"What is undertaking?" Rubee wasn't sure she liked the sound of this.

"Undertaking is carrying our beloved sisters who have passed away out of the hive. They cannot stay inside here. Beehives are one of the cleanest environments found in nature. We must keep everything sanitary so everyone will stay healthy. It is a very important job, Rubee I hope you take it seriously."

"I will, Beeatrice. I will work hard and be a good steward of my … our… time." The young bee smiled warmly at her sister.

"Very good!" Beeatrice rubbed her forelegs together. "I guess I better bee on my way then. I'm off to start my new job, Rubee. I will see you this evening!"

Sanitary—Very clean and free from things that can cause sickness.

Rubee was sad to see her big sister leave but she knew that Beeatrice was just as important to the colony as everyone else, and the food she would bring in would feed many bees. She watched Beeatrice climb down the frame and out the door far below. She said a quick prayer asking God to protect her sister while she was outside, flying in that great big world looking for tasty treats. One day that would be Rubee's job. She sighed and turned back to the frame. "Time to start my new job!" she announced and went busily to work.

And whatever you do, do it heartily, as to the Lord and not to men, knowing that from the Lord you will receive the reward of the inheritance; for you serve the Lord Christ.

Colossians 3:23-24 (NKJV)

As each one has received a special gift, employ it in serving one another as good stewards of the manifold grace of God.

1 Peter 4:10 (NASB 1995)

Blessed is that servant whom the master finds doing his job when he comes.

Luke 12:43 (CSB)

Don't miss out on book 1!

www.ingramcontent.com/pod-product-compliance
Lightning Source LLC
Chambersburg PA
CBHW040438150626
46551CB00023B/116